D0425814

Tom and Ricky
and the
Unlucky Number
Mystery

Bob Wright

High Noon Books
Novato, California

Cover Design and Illustrations: Herb Heidinger

Glossary: trouble, stolen, engine, telephone

International Standard Book Number: 0-87879-400-X

3 2 1 0 9 8 7
0 9 8 7 6 5 4 3 2

Contents

CHAPTER 1

Car Trouble

Tom stopped his bike. He and Ricky were going to go to Eddie's house.

"Ricky, are you ready?" Tom called out.

Ricky was with his dad. They were next to Ricky's dad's car.

"I'm helping my dad," Ricky called back.

"Helping your dad? What's going on? I thought we were going to Eddie's," Tom said.

"The car hasn't been working right," Ricky answered.

"What's the trouble? Maybe I can help," Tom said.

"I don't think you can help," Ricky's dad said.

"The car hasn't been running right. My dad has been trying to fix it for two weeks," Ricky said.

"What are you going to do?" Tom asked.

"I'm going to drive over to Mr. Cord's Car Shop. He sells engines there. I'll talk with him," Ricky's dad said.

"Are you going with your dad?" Tom asked.

"Do you need me, Dad?" Ricky asked.

"No," his dad answered.

"Great!" Ricky said.

"You and Tom can go over and see Eddie. But don't stay too long. I may need you later," Ricky's dad said.

"OK," Ricky said.

Ricky's dad got in the car. He started for Mr. Cord's Car Shop. The car wasn't running very well. But he was able to drive it.

"Come on. Let's get going over to Eddie's house," Tom said.

"Let me call Eddie. I'll tell him we're on our way," Ricky said. He started to go into the house.

All of a sudden, Tom and Ricky heard the phone. It was ringing.

"I bet that's Eddie," Tom said.

Ricky ran into the house. He picked up the phone. "Hello," he said.

"The cherries are ripe," a man said.

"What did you say?" Ricky asked.

"The cherries are ripe," the man said again.

"Is this Eddie?" Ricky asked.

Then the man hung up.

"That's funny," Ricky said. Then he called Eddie. "Eddie?" Ricky asked.

"Is this Ricky?" Eddie asked.

"It sure is. Did you just call me?" Ricky asked.

"No. Why?" Eddie asked.

"Oh, nothing. Tom and I will be right over," Ricky said.

Ricky went back outside.

"What took so long?" Tom asked.

"I got a funny call," Ricky said.

*"When I answered the phone,
a man told me some cherries were ripe."*

"What was funny about it?" Tom asked.

"When I answered the phone, a man told me some cherries were ripe," Ricky said.

"Are you kidding?" Tom asked.

"No. That's just what he said," Ricky answered.

"Do you think it was Eddie?" Tom asked.

"No, it wasn't. I called Eddie. He said he didn't call. He said he was waiting for us," Ricky said.

"Oh, well. Let's get going to Eddie's. Someone called the wrong number," Tom said.

Ricky got on his bike. The two of them started for Eddie's house.

CHAPTER 2

A Stolen Engine

Ricky's dad got back from Mr. Cord's Car Shop.
He parked the car in front of the house. Just then
Tom, Ricky, and Eddie got there on their bikes.

"What's up, Dad?" Ricky asked.

"Mr. Cord looked at the engine. He says it
can't be fixed. We need a new engine," his dad
answered.

"How many miles do you have on it?" Eddie
asked.

"About 150,000," Ricky's dad answered.

"That's a lot. My dad had to get a new engine. He only had 100,000 miles on his," Eddie said.

"I spent a lot of time on the car, Eddie. I take good care of it. But I think it is time for a new engine," Ricky's dad said.

"Can you still drive it?" Ricky asked.

"Yes. I can still drive it. But, it could give out on me at any time," Ricky's dad answered.

"When are you going to have the new engine put in?" Ricky asked.

"Mr. Cord said to come back in two hours. A truck with new engines is going to be there very soon," his dad answered.

"Can we help?" Tom asked.

"You sure can. Why don't you boys go back to Mr. Cord's shop? Let me know when the truck gets there. Then I can take the car in," Ricky's dad said.

"That's a good idea. We won't have to wait long," Tom said.

"And we can look at all the other things," Eddie said.

The three boys got back on their bikes. They started for Front Street.

They parked their bikes in front of Mr. Cord's Car Shop. Then they went in.

"Can I do anything for you boys?" Mr. Cord asked.

"We're waiting for the truck," Ricky said.

"What truck is that?" Mr. Cord asked.

"The truck with the engines," Ricky answered.

"Oh, that's right. Your dad wants a new engine," Mr. Cord said.

"Right," Ricky answered.

"Well, it will be a long wait," Mr. Cord said.

"What's up?" Ricky asked.

"The truck driver just called me. He was coming in by Bear Lake. It's faster than the other way from Oak Falls. He was tired. He stopped to rest and fell asleep," Mr. Cord said.

"There are a lot of hills and trees up by Bear Lake. Not many people live there," Eddie said.

"That's right," Mr. Cord said.

"What about the engines?" Ricky asked.

"The driver fell asleep. When he woke up he checked the truck. All the engines were gone," Mr. Cord said.

"You mean that someone took them?" Ricky asked.

"That's right. There were only six. But they were all taken off the truck," Mr. Cord said.

"What would someone do with six new engines?" Tom asked.

"Sell them," Mr. Cord said.

"In our town?" Tom asked.

"No. I don't think here. This town is too small. This is the only car shop in town. Everyone gets new engines here," Mr. Cord said.

"Where would they go?" Eddie asked.

"I think they might take the engines back to Oak Falls. That's a much bigger city. It would be easier to sell them there," Mr. Cord said.

"Have you called Sergeant Collins?" Tom asked.

"I sure have. He said he would call the police in Oak Falls," Mr. Cord said.

"We better go back and tell your dad," Tom said to Ricky.

"We'll see you later," Ricky said.

"Tell your dad I'll let him know when more new engines are on their way," Mr. Cord said.

"OK," Ricky said. Then the three boys started back to Ricky's house.

CHAPTER 3

Another Call

Tom, Ricky, and Eddie rushed back to Ricky's house. They saw Ricky's dad. He was still working on the car.

"What's up, boys?" he asked.

"You won't get that new engine today," Ricky said.

"Why not? Is the truck late?" his dad asked.

"The engines were stolen from the truck," Ricky said.

"Stolen off the truck? Where?" he asked.

"Up near Bear Lake. The truck driver stopped to rest. When he woke up, the engines were gone," Ricky said.

"There aren't a lot of cars on those roads by Bear Lake. It must have been easy for someone to take those engines," Ricky's dad said.

All of a sudden the phone started to ring.

"Ricky, your mother is out. My hands are full of oil. Will you answer the phone?" Ricky's dad asked.

"Sure," Ricky said. He ran into the house.

"Hello," Ricky said.

"I told you the cherries are ripe. Where are you?" a man asked.

"The cherries? They're ripe?" Ricky asked.

"That's what I said. Come and get them,"

the man said. Then he hung up.

Ricky went back outside.

"Who was it?" his dad asked.

"Who was it?" his dad asked.

"I don't know. A man calling about some cherries," Ricky said.

"Didn't he call before?" Tom asked.

"Yes. It was the same man," Ricky said.

"Why didn't you tell him he had the wrong number?" Eddie asked.

"I was going to. But he hung up before I could tell him that," Ricky said.

"What do you want to do now?" Tom asked.

"Let's go over to Mr. West's Video Store. Maybe he has some new games," Eddie said.

"Don't you boys take too much of Mr. West's time," Ricky's dad said.

"We'll just look around," Ricky said.

The boys got back on their bikes. They started for Front Street again.

"Look. There is Sergeant Collins' car. He's parked in front of Mr. West's store," Eddie called out.

The three boys got off their bikes. They could see Sergeant Collins in the store. He was talking to Mr. West. Then he came outside.

"Hi, Sergeant Collins," Ricky said.

"What are you three going to do today?" the Sergeant asked.

"We were going to help my dad. Mr. Cord was going to put a new engine in our car. But the engines were stolen," Ricky said.

"That's right. They were. I've talked to the police in Oak Falls. They're on the look-out for the six engines," the Sergeant said.

"Who took them?" Ricky asked.

"I don't know. The police in Oak Falls think there is a gang there. That gang robs trucks. They seem to rob the ones going near Bear Lake," the Sergeant said.

"Is Mr. Cord the only one in town who has had trouble?" Ricky asked.

"No, he isn't. Mr. West was waiting for some new video games. They never got here," Sergeant Collins said.

"Was the truck that had his games coming from Oak Falls?" Ricky asked.

"It sure was," the Sergeant answered.

"This sure has been a funny week in town," Eddie said.

"How's that?" the Sergeant asked.

"Mr. Cord doesn't get his engines. Mr. West doesn't get his video games. And Ricky gets funny calls about cherries," Eddie said.

"Cherries? Tell me about those calls," Sergeant Collins said.

CHAPTER 4

A Wrong Number

Sergeant Collins looked at Ricky. He wanted to know about the telephone calls.

"What's this about cherries, Ricky?" Sergeant Collins asked.

"I don't know. I got two calls today. Each time the same man said the cherries are ripe," Ricky answered.

"Did the man say anything else?" the Sergeant asked.

"He just hung up on me," Ricky said.

"What are you thinking?" Eddie asked.

"Something is wrong about all of this," the Sergeant said.

"How's that?" Tom asked.

"This isn't the time of year for cherries," the Sergeant said.

"That's right. I read that cherries are picked in May and June. You can't pick them now," Eddie said.

"Right! I think the man was trying to say that something else was ready. I think it was a code," the Sergeant said.

"But why was he calling me?" Ricky asked.

"I bet he had the wrong number," the Sergeant said.

"You mean he wasn't trying to talk to Ricky? He was trying to talk to someone else?" Tom asked.

"That's right," the Sergeant said.

"Do you think this has anything to do with the stolen engines and video games?" Ricky asked.

"It sure could have," the Sergeant said.

"What do we do now?" Ricky asked.

"Go back home. You might get another call. See if you can find anything out when he calls," the Sergeant said.

"If he calls, what do we do?" Tom asked.

"Let me know right away," the Sergeant answered.

"Come on. Let's get back to my house," Ricky said.

Sergeant Collins got into his car and left.

Tom, Ricky, and Eddie rode back to Ricky's house.

They all ran in and sat by the phone.

"What's going on?" Ricky's dad asked.

"There's a lot of trouble in town. Mr. Cord didn't get his engines. Mr. West didn't get his new video games. Sergeant Collins thinks the same gang stole them," Ricky answered.

"Why does he think that?" his dad asked.

"He's not sure. But both trucks were robbed near Bear Lake. And both trucks were coming from Oak Falls," Ricky answered.

"What are you boys going to do?" his dad asked.

"I might get another call about cherries," Ricky said.

"How do you know that man will call again? You could be here a long time," Ricky's dad said.

"Sergeant Collins thinks the cherries are ripe means something else," Eddie said.

"And we think the man calling here has the wrong number. So he might call again," Ricky said.

"OK. I'll let you boys work this out. I'll be out in the yard," Ricky's dad said.

"We could be here a long time," Tom said.

"I have an idea," Eddie said.

CHAPTER 5

Eddie's Idea

Eddie looked at Tom and Ricky. He was thinking. Tom and Ricky waited for him to say something.

"Well, what is it? What's your idea?" Tom asked.

"Ricky, your phone number is 555-1234, right?" Eddie asked.

"Right," Ricky answered.

"No one could get mixed up with 555, right?" Eddie asked.

"Right," Ricky said.

"Then someone had to get mixed up with the last four numbers, right?" Eddie asked.

"Everyone in this town has a number that starts with 555," Tom said.

"That's right," Eddie said.

"Do you mean we have to call everyone in town and say the cherries are ripe?" Tom asked.

"No. This is what I'm saying. No one could mix up 555. But someone could mix up the last four numbers," Eddie said.

"There are still a lot of numbers with 1, 2, 3, 4, in them," Ricky said.

"Tom. Say this back to me. 333-9482," Eddie said.

"333-9....9..... I forgot," Tom said.

"Try again," Eddie said.

"333-9....9....8....2....4...." Tom said.

"You got the numbers. But they're mixed up," Eddie said.

"I see what you mean," Ricky yelled. He jumped up.

"Well tell me what's going on," Tom said.

"Eddie thinks 1-2-3-4 are in the number, but they're mixed up. Just like you did. Eddie also thinks the right number starts with 555-1," Ricky said.

"You got it," Eddie said.

"I'm still mixed up. I just don't get it," Tom said.

"Look, Tom. We'll write all the ways we can use 2-3-4 in a telephone number. That will be easy," Ricky said.

Ricky gave Eddie a paper and pencil. Eddie wrote all these numbers on the paper.

555 - 1423

555 - 1432

555 - 1324

555 - 1342

555 - 1243

555 - 1234

"I think it has to be one of those numbers," Eddie said.

"I think I get it. But what do we do now?" Tom asked.

"Let's call each one," Eddie said.

"What would we say to the people who answer?" Tom asked.

"I think it has to be one of those numbers,"
Eddie said.

"We could say that the cherries are ripe," Eddie said.

"And then what?" Ricky asked.

"I don't know," Eddie answered.

"I think we better go and see Sergeant Collins. Let's see what he says. There might be trouble if we call all those people," Ricky said.

"That's a good idea. Come on. Let's get going," Tom said.

"Be sure to take that paper with the phone numbers," Ricky called out to Eddie.

They ran out of the house to their bikes. They rode up Page Street. Then they went down Front Street to the police station.

CHAPTER 6

Another Idea

Sergeant Collins was on the phone. But he saw the three boys come running into the police station. "Thank you for calling. We'll look into it," he said. Then he put the phone down.

"We're on to something," Tom said.

"On to what?" the Sergeant asked.

"The stolen engines and the video games," Ricky said.

"What's new? Did you get another call?" the Sergeant asked.

"No. We waited. But there wasn't another call," Tom said.

"But Eddie had an idea. Tell him, Eddie," Ricky said.

Eddie told Sergeant Collins his idea. He showed him the paper with numbers. The Sergeant looked at the numbers.

"I think you have a good idea. Let's give this a try. I'm glad you didn't call any of these numbers. Let me see what I can find out," the Sergeant said.

"What will you do? Will you call the numbers?" Tom asked.

"I think I should. But you know what?" the Sergeant said.

"What's that?" Ricky asked.

"When you came in, I was on the phone. A man called me. He lives up at Bear Lake. He said there has been a blue truck up by the lake," the Sergeant said.

"What's wrong with that?" Eddie asked.

"He only saw that truck on the days the engines and video games were stolen," the Sergeant said.

"Do you think that blue truck has something to do with the stolen engines and games?" Ricky asked.

"It might," the sergeant said.

"Let's call those numbers. I want to know if I'm right," Eddie said.

Sergeant Collins picked up the phone. He started to call the numbers on Eddie's list. Each time someone answered, he said, "The cherries are ripe." The first, 555-1423, was a rest home. The next number, 555-1432, was not working.

Then he called 555-1324. "The cherries are ripe," Sergeant Collins said.

"It's about time. What took so long? I'll be right there," the man said. Then he hung up.

Sergeant Collins put the phone down. "Eddie, you were right. Someone did get the number mixed up. Someone got the 3 and the 2 mixed up. That's why the man was calling you, Ricky. He meant to call 555-1324, but he called 555-1234," the Sergeant said.

"Now what do we do?" Ricky asked.

"Now I'll call the phone company. We'll find out who has that phone number," the Sergeant said.

He picked up the phone. "Get me the phone company," he said. He waited. Then he said, "This is Sergeant Collins at the Police Station. I need a house number for 555-1324. I need it fast," he said. He waited again. Then he said. "Thank you."

"What did you find out?" Ricky asked.

"Let's get going. Come on with me. The house is at 1313 Lake Street," the Sergeant said.

They all ran out to the Sergeant's car.

"We're on our way," the Sergeant said.

CHAPTER 7

Fast Move

Sergeant Collins had to drive fast. He needed to get to 1313 Lake Street right away.

"What do you think we'll find when we get there?" Ricky asked.

"I don't know. We could be wrong. But maybe we're right," the Sergeant said.

"How's that?" Eddie asked.

"The cherries, the stolen things, and the blue truck. Maybe they don't have anything to do with one another," the Sergeant said.

"Why don't you put your red light on?" Tom asked.

"I don't want them to know we're coming," the Sergeant said. He turned on to Lake Street.

Then Ricky yelled, "Look! A blue truck just passed us. It's going the other way!"

"I could be wrong, but I'm going to go after that truck," the Sergeant said.

"Are you going to stop him?" Eddie asked.

"No. I'll stay in back of him. I won't let him know we're after him," the Sergeant said.

Sergeant Collins stayed far in back of the blue truck.

"Look. The truck is going up to Bear Lake," Eddie said.

"Maybe we are right after all," the Sergeant said.

The blue truck started for the hills.

*Sergeant Collins stayed far
in back of the blue truck.*

The roads weren't as good as in town. The truck went slower. Sergeant Collins couldn't stay too close. He had to go slower, too.

"This will be hard now. That truck has to go slow. There aren't many cars. He might see us," Sergeant Collins said.

Then the blue truck turned. It went on to a dirt road.

"I know that dirt road. He will be able to see us if we turn into it. I'll have to stop the car here," the Sergeant said.

He pulled off the road. Then he stopped by some trees. "The trees will hide the police car. That road doesn't go far. Let's just wait here," the Sergeant said.

"What if the truck doesn't come back out this way?" Tom asked.

"It has to. There's no other way it can get out. That dirt road just stops," the Sergeant said.

"What will you do when it comes out?" Ricky asked.

"I'll stop it," the Sergeant said.

"What do you think is going on?" Tom asked.

"I think that blue truck is getting the engines and video games. Then it takes them to another town and sells them," the Sergeant said.

Then Ricky said, "Look! Here it comes!"

The blue truck was coming back out on to the road.

Sergeant Collins started his car. He put on his red light. The truck didn't stop.

"That truck isn't stopping. It's going faster," Ricky said.

"I'll have to get some help." Sergeant Collins picked up his car phone.

"This is Collins. I'm up on Bear Lake Road. I'm after a blue truck. It won't stop. I think it has the stolen engines and video games," the Sergeant said.

"We're on our way," was the answer.

"We're OK now. We're in back of them. Two cars will be in front of them. They'll have to stop," the Sergeant said to the boys.

All of a sudden the truck stopped.

"That was fast," Eddie said.

"You boys stay here. There might be trouble," Sergeant Collins said.

"Look at that! They have engines, tires, stoves—everything," Ricky said.

Sergeant Collins got out of the car. He walked over to the other police who were in front of the truck.

Two men got out of the truck. Sergeant Collins made them open the back of the truck.

"Look at that! They have engines, tires, stoves—everything," Ricky said.

One policeman got in the truck. The other one took the two men to his car. Sergeant Collins came back to his car. "That's the gang we've been looking for," he said.

"They had a lot of things in the truck," Tom said.

"This has been going on for a long time," the Sergeant said.

"Is that the gang?" Eddie asked.

"No. There are more. But we'll get them, thanks to you boys. You were right to tell me about that call. The cherries meant to come and get all those things," the Sergeant said.

"Well, now my dad can get his car fixed," Ricky said.

"You know what?" Tom asked.

"What's that?" Ricky answered.

"The next time someone tells you the cherries are ripe, tell him to go and get them at the market," Tom said.

F   Wright, Bob.
Wri   Tom and Ricky and
         the unlucky number
         mystery

PERMA-BOUND

DATE DUE			

F   Wright, Bob.
Wri   Tom and Ricky and
         the unlucky number
         mystery

DATE DUE	BORROWER'S NAME	RM. NO.
SE1 4 '93	Kevin Stanley	4A